DreamWorks

HOW TO TRAIN YOUR

DRAGON

HOMECOMING

ADAPTED BY **MAY NAKAMURA**

ILLUSTRATED BY **PATRICK SPAZIANTE**

Simon Spotlight

New York London Toronto Sydney New Delhi

SIMON SPOTLIGHT
An imprint of Simon & Schuster Children's Publishing Division
1230 Avenue of the Americas, New York, New York 10020
This Simon Spotlight edition October 2019

For information about special discounts for bulk purchases, please contact Simon & Schuster
Special Sales at 1-866-506-1949 or business@simonandschuster.com.
Manufactured in the United States of America 0819 LAK
2 4 6 8 10 9 7 5 3 1
ISBN 978-1-5344-5235-0
ISBN 978-1-5344-5236-7 (eBook)

In New Berk, it was almost Snoggletog, the best time of the year. The villagers strolled through the town square, admiring the holiday decorations and holiday shops. They sang Viking carols and drank yak-nog. Everyone was happy.

The Snoggletog season reminded Hiccup of Toothless, his best friend. On Snoggletog Eve, Hiccup used to make Toothless's favorite meal: lake trout with a side of sea trout on a bed of brook trout. Toothless loved trout!

Ten years had passed since the Vikings and dragons agreed to live apart, but Hiccup still caught trout every Snoggletog.

Hiccup asked his children, Zephyr and Nuffink, if they wanted to help him cook the trout this year. "Dragons are wonderful. They are our friends," he said.

"No, they are monsters," Zephyr answered. "They have razor-sharp teeth and huge claws. I don't want to become a dragon's dessert!"

"Me neither," Nuffink agreed.

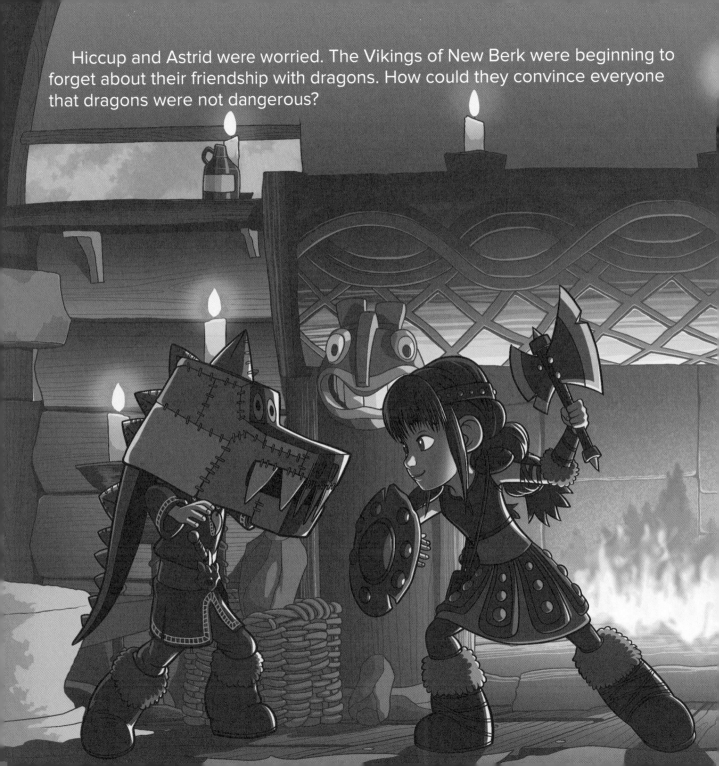

Hiccup and Astrid were worried. The Vikings of New Berk were beginning to forget about their friendship with dragons. How could they convince everyone that dragons were not dangerous?

Astrid suggested hosting a pageant, which had been a Snoggletog tradition back when she and Hiccup were kids. "We could put on a play about how Vikings and dragons became friends," she said.

Hiccup thought it was a great idea.

Hiccup asked Gobber to write the script. Together, they decided that the pageant would include all the history that Viking children should know.

"This pageant is going to be just what New Berk needs," Gobber said. "To honor dragons and of course . . . to honor my great friend, Stoick."

In his workshop, Hiccup began to build a life-size mechanical puppet of Toothless. He wanted to make it look just like the real Toothless so that Zephyr and Nuffink would fall in love with it.

Meanwhile, in the Hidden World, Toothless was teaching his family about humans. He drew pictures of Hiccup and New Berk in the sand.

The pictures fascinated the Night Lights. Eager to see New Berk with their own eyes, they snuck out of the Hidden World and took off into the night sky!

Back in New Berk, Tuffnut rehearsed his lines for the pageant. He was playing the role of Hiccup.

"A dragon is coming. Aaah. Help me!" Tuffnut cried. Then he threw up his arms and ran off the stage.

"That's not like me at all!" Hiccup complained, but Astrid and Gobber thought it was perfect.

Then they held auditions for the role of Stoick. Fishlegs delivered a wonderful performance. In the end, however, Gobber insisted on playing the part!

Finally, Snoggletog was here. The whole village, including Zephyr and Nuffink, gathered to watch the pageant.

Little did they know that the Night Lights were watching the pageant too! Soon, Toothless and the Light Fury joined them. They scolded the Night Lights for flying off to New Berk, but before they could head back to the Hidden World, the pageant began.

The Toothless puppet, handled by Hiccup, entered the stage. "There he is: the Night Fury, in all his awesome glory," Gobber recited as Stoick.

The audience was mesmerized by the realistic puppet. Hiccup smiled from inside the puppet. Everything was going perfectly.

Then Gobber stumbled and knocked over a torch. Suddenly the whole stage was burning!

In the chaos of the fire, Hiccup lost control of the mechanical Toothless puppet. It roared and started storming toward the audience.

Zephyr and Nuffink screamed. Their worst nightmare was coming to life!

The real Toothless launched into action. He flew through the smoke as the puppet marched toward the edge of the stage with Hiccup still inside.

Toothless dove and caught Hiccup just in time. In the smoky haze, Hiccup couldn't tell who had saved him.

The puppet was completely ruined, so Toothless, disguised by the smoke, stepped onto the stage to finish the pageant himself.

"Let man and dragon be forever bonded in trust and love," Gobber recited. He reached out and touched Toothless's snout.

The villagers burst into applause. In the end, the pageant was a hit!

"That was amazing!" Nuffink cheered. But there was one person who still wasn't convinced. "It was just Dad in a suit," said Zephyr.

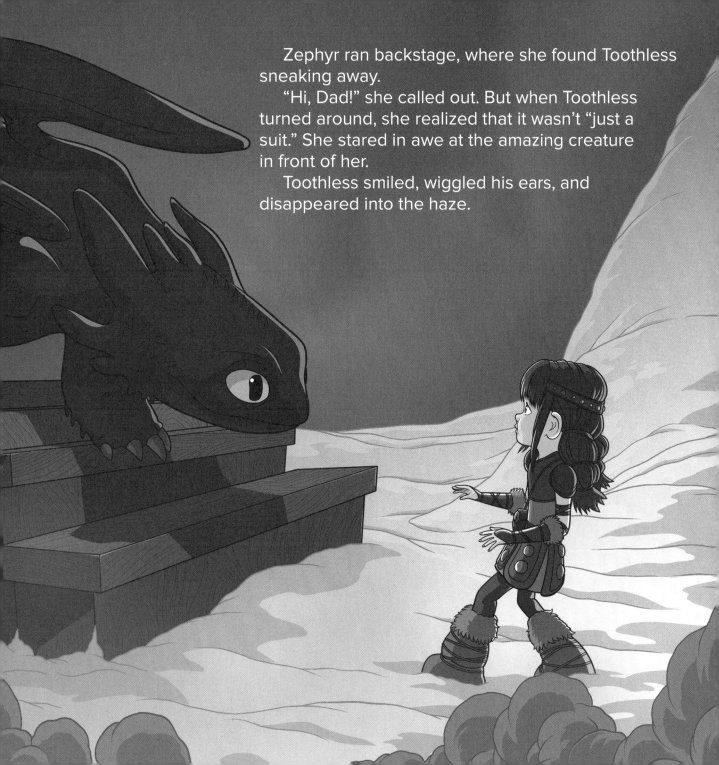

Zephyr ran backstage, where she found Toothless sneaking away.

"Hi, Dad!" she called out. But when Toothless turned around, she realized that it wasn't "just a suit." She stared in awe at the amazing creature in front of her.

Toothless smiled, wiggled his ears, and disappeared into the haze.

On the way home, Zephyr bubbled with excitement. "I love dragons! I love Toothless! Why didn't you tell me that you were actually going to bring him here?" "What is she talking about?" Hiccup asked. Astrid shrugged.

When the family arrived at home, they were shocked to see a glowing crystal from the Hidden World in their living room.

"And look!" Astrid cried. "The bowl of trout is empty!"

They all rushed to the window just in time to see the dragons flying high across the night sky.

Astrid turned to Hiccup with a knowing look in her eye.

Seeing Toothless was the perfect Snoggletog gift for Hiccup. That night he went to sleep with a big grin on his face. Not only did he get to see his best friend, but his children now also knew that the dragons are beautiful friends.

"Maybe it's our turn to visit them," said Astrid.

Happy Snoggletog!